Flubby Will
Not
Play with That

For Flubby Morris—JEM

W

PENGUIN WORKSHOP
An Imprint of Penguin Random House LLC, New York

Penguin supports copyright. Copyright fuels creativity, encourages diverse voices, promotes free speech, and creates a vibrant culture. Thank you for buying an authorized edition of this book and for complying with copyright laws by not reproducing, scanning, or distributing any part of it in any form without permission. You are supporting writers and allowing Penguin to continue to publish books for every reader.

Copyright © 2019 by Jennifer Morris. All rights reserved. Published by Penguin Workshop, an imprint of Penguin Random House LLC, New York. PENGUIN and PENGUIN WORKSHOP are trademarks of Penguin Books Ltd, and the W colophon is a registered trademark of Penguin Random House LLC. Manufactured in China.

Visit us online at www.penguinrandomhouse.com.

Library of Congress Cataloging-in-Publication Data is available upon request.

ISBN 9781524787783   10 9 8 7 6 5 4 3 2 1

Flubby Will **Not** Play with That

Zzzzz

by J. E. Morris

Penguin Workshop

I have toys for Flubby.

I have lots of toys for Flubby.

This toy sings.

Flubby, go get it!

It is fine. I have another toy.

This toy rolls.

It is fine. I have another toy.

This toy swings.

It is fine. I have another toy.

Yawn

This is the last toy.

This is the best one.

Flubby will love this toy.

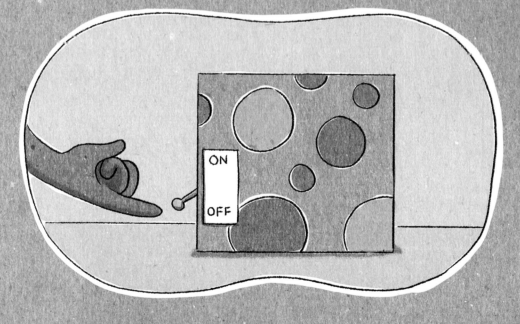

Oh dear.

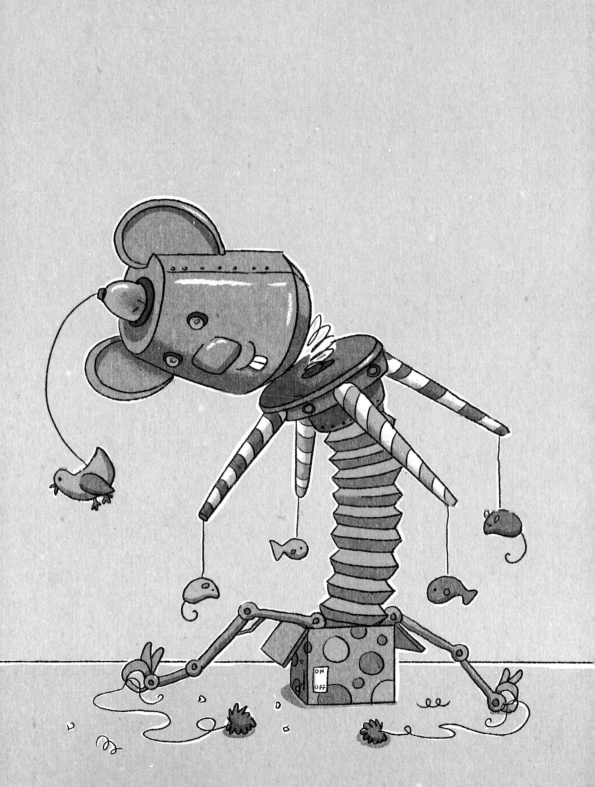

There are no more toys.

Sorry, Flubby.

TAP
TAP

29

There *was* a toy
for Flubby after all!